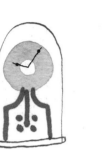    

For Adam, who is always on time*

With special thanks to Chris and Veronique

First published 2018 by Macmillan Children's Books
an imprint of Pan Macmillan
20 New Wharf Road, London N1 9RR
Associated companies throughout the world
www.panmacmillan.com

ISBN 978-1-5098-5233-8 (HB)
ISBN 978-1-5098-5234-5 (PB)

Text and illustrations copyright © Nicola Kent 2018

The right of Nicola Kent to be identified as the author and illustrator of this work
has been asserted by her in accordance with the Copyright, Designs and Patents Act 1988.

1 3 5 7 9 8 6 4 2

A CIP catalogue record for this book
is available from the British Library.

Printed in China

*This may or may not be true.

Bye love!

Vera Jewel
is Late for School

honk honk

Nicola Kent

MACMILLAN CHILDREN'S BOOKS

Bye love!

On Monday morning, Vera Jewel
Hopped on her bike to ride to school.

honk
honk

But a great big spike,

Meant a broken bike.

And Vera Jewel . . .

. . . was late for school.

Vera Jewel felt quite forlorn.
She loved that bike, those wheels, that horn!
Scratched her head . . . what instead?

Skateboard?

Scooter?

Unicorn?

Tuesday morning, Vera Jewel

Rules
No running
No jumping
Bouncing's fine

Yum

School

Was bouncing past the paddling pool.

uh oh!

QUACK!

Banana skin . . .

And Vera Jewel . . .

Squeeze

. . . was late for school.

Sorry Sir

Maths
on the
Go!

Vera!

Wednesday morning,
Vera Jewel

Built a special travel tool.

But what a pain . . .   She's home again!

And Vera Jewel was late for school.

Thursday morning, Vera Jewel
Bought her neighbour's champion mule.

Off they dashed . . .

. . . Vera crashed!

And Vera Jewel
was late for school.

Friday morning, Vera Jewel
Filled a plane with rocket fuel.

Bye love!

Vera soon . . .

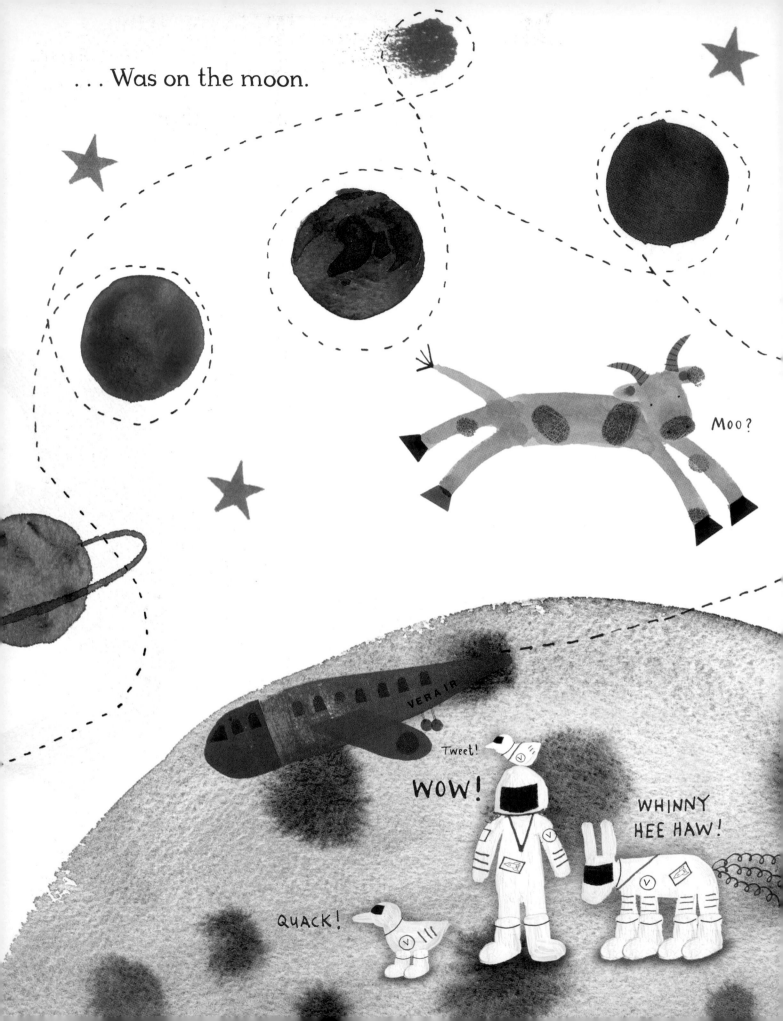

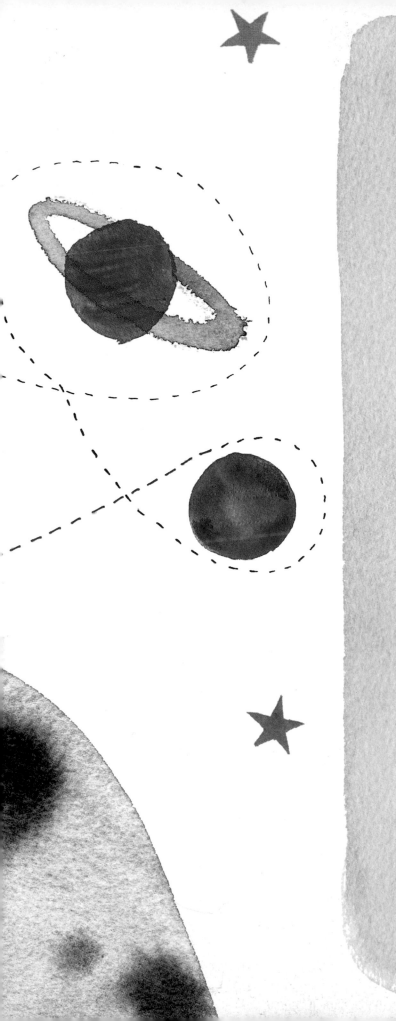

And Vera Jewel
was late for school.

Sorry sir

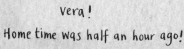
vera !
Home time was half an hour ago!

There's only
one thing
for it

Friday night and Vera Jewel   Camped outside the door
to school.

She woke on time,   Was first in line . . .

...On Saturday. Oh Vera Jewel!

Now Vera's feeling really blue.
It seems there's nothing left to do!
Why did that spike
Have to break her bike?

But wait . . .

... Eureka! She's got it! Phew!

100% Organic mega-nourishing mobile meadow for jumping cows at rest

Recycled travel tool handlebars for accurate steering

Super-comfy ultra-padded bottom-friendly seat

Moon rock-armoured spike-proof speedy wheels for punctual girls

120 miles per hour running machine for champion mules in training

VERAIR

Plane tail for extra whoosh

Pure pond water with no artificial additives for ducks in transit

Helmet with built-in luxury fleece-lined nest for birds a-laying

All through Sunday and half the night,
Vera works to fix her plight.

And Monday morning, what a surprise!
Her teacher can't believe his eyes.

Wow Vera!

Morning Sir!

It's Vera Jewel . . .
ON TIME FOR SCHOOL!
And her special bike is . . .

SUPERSIZE!

It's super fast, it's super cool,
This bicycle's the talk of school.
And when class ends, now all her friends
Love riding home with Vera Jewel!

New!
SPECIAL
CARRIAGE
for special guests

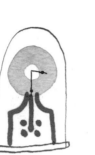

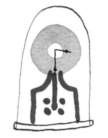

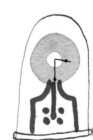

Headteacher's Award

To: Vera Jewel

For never giving up!

Signed